GW00864409

MAMGU'S CAMPERVAN

**and the Knights
in Shining Armour**

MAMGU'S CAMPERVAN

and the Knights
in Shining Armour

Wendy White

Illustrated by
Helen Flook

Gomer

First published in 2018
by Gomer Press, Llandysul, Ceredigion SA44 4JL
www.gomer.co.uk

ISBN: 978 1 78562 254 0

A CIP record for this title is available from the British Library.

© Copyright: Wendy White, 2018
© Illustration Copyright: Helen Flook, 2018

Wendy White and Helen Flook have asserted their moral right
under the Copyright, Designs and Patents Act, 1988
to be identified as author and illustrator of this work.

All rights reserved. No part of this book may be reproduced,
stored in a retrieval system, or transmitted in any form
or by any means, electronic, electrostatic, magnetic tape,
mechanical, photocopying, recording or otherwise
without permission in writing from the above publishers.

This book is published with the financial support
of the Welsh Books Council.

Printed and bound in Wales at
Gomer Press, Llandysul, Ceredigion

Chapter 1

'Look, Mam-gu!' Betsi Wyn called, as she pointed out of the window. 'The sun's smiling at last.'

'About time too,' Mam-gu said. 'It's the first sunny day of the holidays.'

Betsi Wyn hopped up and down. 'You promised we could get Heulwen out once it stopped raining.'

Mam-gu nodded. 'I did. And today's the perfect day to take her out of the garage.'

'Hooray!' Betsi Wyn cheered. 'I love Heulwen. Can we go and get her now?'

Mam-gu smiled. 'In a minute. Let's tidy up these breakfast things and make ourselves a picnic.'

Betsi Wyn helped Mam-gu find all the things they needed – Welsh cakes, milk, teabags and a big bottle of water. Then they made a stack of cheese sandwiches and packed everything into a cool-bag.

Mam-gu found the key to the garage in the kitchen drawer. 'Come on, Betsi Wyn,' she said. 'Let's see if that old camper van will start for us.'

Once Mam-gu had hauled open the garage doors, Betsi Wyn rushed inside and gave the van a hug. 'How are you, Heulwen? I've missed you all winter. But now it's spring again and we're going to take you out.'

Mam-gu smiled and opened Heulwen's door. She lifted the bag of food into the back of the van then climbed up onto the driver's seat. 'Right,' she said. 'Let's get started.' And she turned the key in the ignition.

Heulwen's engine made a sad chug-chug sound.

'Oh no,' Betsi Wyn said. 'Isn't she working?'

Mam-gu rubbed the dashboard. 'Heulwen's always a bit slow to start after the winter. I'll just give her a minute or two, and then I'll try again.'

But the van didn't start the second time Mam-gu tried either.

Betsi Wyn stroked Heulwen's bumper. 'Don't you want to get out of this garage?' she whispered. 'Don't you want to come for a picnic?'

Mam-gu turned the key once more and with a loud groan, the engine rattled into life.

'Let's get going before she stops again,' Mam-gu called. 'Come on, jump in – quick!'

Chapter 2

The camper van soon stopped chugging once it was on the road.

'She's going along very smoothly now,' Mam-gu said. 'She loves the sunshine.'

Betsi Wyn nodded. 'That's why you called her Heulwen, isn't it?'

'That's right,' Mam-gu agreed. 'Because *heulwen* means sunshine... and because she's yellow, of course.'

They passed lots of camper vans like Mam-gu's, and every time they passed one, Betsi Wyn and Mam-gu waved excitedly. The people in the other vans waved back cheerfully too.

'This lovely weather's brought everyone out,' Mam-gu said. She sighed happily. 'This is the life.'

'Yes,' said Betsi Wyn. 'It's perfect.'

They'd been driving a while when Betsi Wyn asked, 'Where are we going, Mam-gu?'

'You know, I hadn't thought about that. Where would you like to go?'

'To Scotland,' Betsi Wyn said. 'I want to visit Aunty Mair and her new baby, Tirion.'

Mam-gu smiled. 'Me too. That would be lovely. But we haven't got time to drive all the way to Scotland today. What about doing something here in Wales?'

Betsi Wyn thought for a minute. 'We could visit a castle. We've got plenty of those in Wales.

And we could take some photos to send to Aunty Mair.'

'That's a wonderful idea,' Mam-gu said. 'Now all we have to do is find a castle to visit.'

'You drive around,' Betsi Wyn said, 'and I'll tell you when I spot one.'

Chapter 3

It didn't take long before Betsi Wyn shouted, '*Castell*, Mam-gu!' She was pointing to a castle in the distance with high walls and tumbledown towers. The castle was on a hill next to a river. 'Can we go there? That castle looks just right.'

'Oh yes,' Mam-gu said. 'That *castell* is perfect. Let's drive into the town and find somewhere to park.' And she turned the van towards the little town centre.

As they walked from the car park to the castle they could hear lots of cheering. There were flags flying from the castle's towers.

'What's going on?' Betsi Wyn asked.

Mam-gu pointed to a board at the side of the road. 'That sign says there's a medieval fair at the castle today.'

'What's a medieval fair?'

'I don't exactly know,' Mam-gu said. 'Shall we take a peep through the castle gate and find out?'

The big square of grass inside the castle was full of colourful tents. There were people dressed in olden-day clothes. Some were wearing brown trousers and grubby shirts, and some wore long dresses that had mud on the hems. But a few of the people were dressed beautifully, like princesses and princes. And there was even a group of people in suits of armour.

'This is wonderful,' Betsi Wyn said. 'Please can we go in, Mam-gu?'

Mam-gu laughed. '*Wrth gwrs*. Of course. But we'd better buy our tickets first.'

Chapter 4

It was great fun at the castle. There was a deep dungeon that Betsi Wyn and Mam-gu peered down into, and lots of winding staircases to climb. They could even walk along the top of the castle walls.

'Let's go carefully,' Mam-gu gasped. They were very high up. 'And hold onto the handrail.'

They could see all around the town. 'Look,' Betsi Wyn said. 'There's Heulwen.'

Mam-gu peered into the distance. 'Oh yes,' she said, when she finally spotted the yellow van. 'There she is, waiting for us.' Mam-gu took her mobile phone from her pocket. 'Now, let's get a photo of you with Heulwen in the background, and we can send it to Aunty Mair.'

From the top of the walls they had a good view of all the interesting things going on inside the castle too. Lots of people had gathered in the very centre and some were trying on pieces of armour.

'Look! Those people are pretending to be knights,' Betsi Wyn said. 'Can we do that?'

'I don't see why not,' Mam-gu said. 'Let's go down and see.'

The man who helped Betsi Wyn try on armour was very friendly. He put some chain mail on her shoulders and a shiny piece of metal around her neck. 'That's the collar this rests on,' he explained, lifting a huge metal helmet onto Betsi Wyn's head.

'Stay where you are,' Mam-gu told her, 'and I'll take a photo of you.'

'Don't worry,' Betsi Wyn said through the gap in the helmet, 'I'm not going anywhere. I can't move a muscle! How did people walk in this thing?'

The man laughed. 'I suppose they got used to it. After all, it was their job to wear armour and to go around helping people.'

'Can I take it off now, please?' Betsi Wyn asked. 'I don't think I'd have liked being a knight after all.'

'Well, you might like being an archer,' the man said, as he helped Betsi Wyn out of the helmet. He pointed to the other side of the castle. 'You can have a try over there.'

Chapter 5

There was a long queue to try out archery, but it was fun watching other people firing arrows at the big round targets. Some people were excellent and almost hit the bullseye. Others weren't quite so good and their arrows ended up in the grass.

Betsi Wyn was very excited when it was her turn. A smiling lady showed her how to hold the bow. It was a bit tricky. Betsi Wyn missed the target with her first arrow, but when she tried again she hit one of the circles at the edge of the board.

'*Da iawn*,' the lady said. 'Very good. Now, line up your next arrow carefully and...'

But before she could finish her sentence, Betsi Wyn's arrow flew to the target and hit the bullseye.

'Wow!' the lady said. 'You're really good at this. Perhaps you should join our archery club.'

Betsi Wyn beamed. 'Did you hear that, Mam-gu?' she said. 'The lady told me I was very good.'

'Yes.' Mam-gu nodded. 'I did hear. And I saw it for myself. I took lots of photos too.'

They were having a lovely time at the castle, but soon their tummies began to rumble.

'There's something cooking over there,' Betsi Wyn said, pointing to a fire with a big pot hanging above it. A lady in a long brown dress was stirring the pot. 'Do you think we can have some of that?'

'Let's go and ask,' Mam-gu said.

Chapter 6

The lady was very pleased that they wanted to try her broth. She ladled it into two wooden bowls and then she gave them each a funny-looking spoon. 'These spoons are made from sheep horns,' she said. 'That's what they used in medieval times.'

Mam-gu laughed. 'Now, there's a novelty!'

But Betsi Wyn didn't like the idea of eating with a sheep's horn.

'You can drink from the bowl instead if you want,' the lady said.

Betsi Wyn was very hungry. She took a big slurp from her bowl. '*Ych a fi!*' she said and she pulled a face. 'Urgh! That soup's horrible.' Then she remembered the lady. Betsi Wyn hadn't meant to say something rude about her cooking, so she gave her a little smile.

Mam-gu spluttered as she tried to swallow her spoonful of broth. 'Goodness,' she said, 'it does taste a little…peculiar.'

The lady nodded. 'It's horrible, isn't it? Soup was made from any old leftovers back then.'

Mam-gu and Betsi Wyn slowly put down their bowls. 'We'll give it a miss, if you don't mind,' Mam-gu said.

'I don't blame you,' said the lady. 'I wouldn't eat it if you paid me.' And she picked up their bowls and tipped their soup back into her big pot.

Mam-gu winked at Betsi Wyn. 'I think it's time we checked on Heulwen and had our sandwiches, don't you?' And they set off for the car park.

Chapter 7

It was lovely sitting in the camper van with the doors open wide. They ate all the sandwiches and Welsh cakes, and Mam-gu boiled water for cups of tea on Heulwen's little stove. By the time they'd finished their picnic, everyone was starting to leave the castle. Betsi Wyn and Mam-gu climbed into the front of the van, and Mam-gu put the key into Heulwen's ignition. But no matter how much she turned the key, the van just wouldn't start.

'Oh no,' Mam-gu said. 'She won't budge. How on earth are we going to get home?'

Betsi Wyn put her chin in her hands. 'And we were having such a lovely day,' she sighed.

Then her head suddenly bounced up. 'Look, Mam-gu.' She was pointing to the castle. 'Here come the knights. The man with the armour said knights help people. Perhaps they can help us.'

'Brilliant thinking, Betsi Wyn!' Mam-gu cried, and she jumped out of the van as quickly as she could and ran off to have a chat with them.

It wasn't long before all the knights were arranged behind the camper van.

'Heave on the count of three,' one of them shouted. '*Un, dau…TRI!*'

They all shoved against Heulwen's bumper and soon she was rolling from one end of the car park to the other.

'Let her clutch out now,' the knight called, and the van rattled into life.

'Quick, Betsi Wyn,' Mam-gu shouted. 'Get in!' And Betsi Wyn clambered into the front seat. '*Diolch yn fawr!* Thank you!' Mam-gu called out of the window. 'You really are our knights in shining armour.'

'*Croeso,*' the knights shouted back, their armour sparkling in the sunshine. 'You're welcome.' And they waved goodbye. '*Hwyl fawr!*'

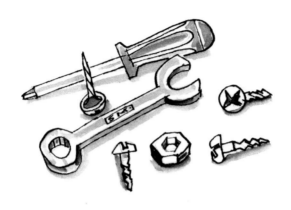

Chapter 8

'What an adventure,' Mam-gu said as they chug-chugged their slow way home.

'Yes,' Betsi Wyn agreed. 'It's been brilliant. And I've got loads of photos of the knights pushing the van. Aunty Mair will love them. Where shall we take Heulwen tomorrow?'

Mam-gu laughed. 'I think we'd better take her to a van mechanic, don't you?'

'Oh,' said Betsi Wyn, sadly. She was

disappointed. She'd been hoping for another adventure.

Mam-gu smiled. 'But then, once she's working properly, we'll take our lovely Heulwen on a trip to see Aunty Mair and your new baby cousin.'

'We'll go to Scotland?' Betsi Wyn said. 'In Heulwen?' She clapped her hands. 'Can we show them our photos when we get there?'

Mam-gu nodded.

'Hooray!' Betsi Wyn shouted, and she waved her arms in the air.

'Hooray!' Mam-gu cheered too, and a pink camper van on the other side of the road tooted its horn at them happily.

Then Betsi Wyn switched on Heulwen's crackly old radio, and she and Mam-gu sang at the very top of their voices all the way home.

The End!

Other Gomer books
by
Wendy White

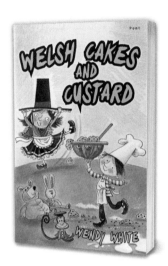